HIGH HOPES
FOR ADDY

ADDY · 1864

BY CONNIE PORTER

ILLUSTRATIONS JOHN THOMPSON
AND DAHL TAYLOR

VIGNETTES SUSAN MCALILEY

THE AMERICAN GIRLS COLLECTION®

Published by Pleasant Company Publications
Previously published in *American Girl*® magazine
© Copyright 1999 by Pleasant Company

Printed in Hong Kong.
99 00 01 02 03 04 05 06 C&C 10 9 8 7 6 5

The American Girls Collection®, Addy®, and Addy Walker®
are trademarks of Pleasant Company.

Edited by Nancy Holyoke and Michelle Jones
Designed by Tricia Doherty and Laura Moberly
Art Directed by Kym Abrams and Laura Moberly

Library of Congress Cataloging-in-Publication Data

Porter, Connie Rose, 1959–
High hopes for Addy / by Connie Porter ;
illustrations by John Thompson, Dahl Taylor ; vignettes by Susan McAliley.
p. cm. — (The American girls collection)
Summary: Addy's new life in Philadelphia in the late 1860s continues to hold
surprises, as she competes in a kite festival and her teacher recommends her for
the Institute for Colored Youth. Includes informational pages about the Institute
for Colored Youth and how to make a kite.

ISBN 1-56247-765-X
1. Afro-Americans—Juvenile fiction. [1. Afro-Americans—Fiction.
2. Kites—Fiction. 3. Schools—Fiction.]
I. Thompson, John, ill. II. Taylor, Dahl, ill. III. Title. IV. Series.
PZ7.P825Hi 1999 [Fic]—dc21 98-40675 CIP AC

The AMERICAN GIRLS COLLECTION™

PICTURE CREDITS

The following organizations have generously given permission to reprint illustrations used in "Looking Back": p. 34—The Library Company of Philadelphia; p. 35—Corbis-Bettmann (top); National Portrait Gallery, Smithsonian Institution/Art Resource, New York (bottom); p. 37—Oberlin College Archive, Oberlin, Ohio; p. 39—The Granger Collection, New York; p. 40—Hampton University's Archival and Museum Collection, Hampton University, Hampton, Virginia; p. 41—Courtesy of Hargrett Rare Book and Manuscript Library/University of Georgia Libraries; p. 42—Photography by Jamie Young.

TABLE OF CONTENTS

ADDY'S FAMILY

POPPA
Addy's father, whose dream gives the family strength.

MOMMA
Addy's mother, whose love helps the family survive.

ADDY
A courageous girl, smart and strong, growing up during the Civil War.

SAM
Addy's sixteen-year-old brother, determined to be free.

ESTHER
Addy's two-year-old sister.

MISS DUNN
*Addy's kind and
patient teacher, who
doesn't like lines to be
drawn between people.*

HARRIET
*Addy's desk partner,
who has the life Addy
thought freedom would
bring to her.*

M'DEAR
*An elderly woman who
befriends Addy.*

MR. AND MRS. GOLDEN
*The owners of the boarding
house where the Walkers live.*

HIGH HOPES
FOR ADDY

Addy sat on the floor, cutting paper for a kite she was making. It was Sunday afternoon, and her whole family—Momma, Poppa, Sam, and Esther—was together in their room in the boarding house. A strong spring breeze blew through the window and made the paper flutter.

"Ain't it something," said Addy, smoothing it down.

"Ain't what something?" asked

Momma. She was sitting at the table with Poppa, cutting scraps of cloth for the kite's tail. Poppa was paring down strips of wood for the frame.

"All that go into making a kite—

 paper, glue, wood, string, cloth, this spool Sam bought me," Addy said.

"Can't none of them fly, but all together they make something that can. It's like they all need each other to do it."

"It's kind of like a riddle," said Sam, who was down on the floor playing with Esther. "One by one they fail, but together they sail."

"I like that riddle," said Poppa. "Lots of things in life is like that."

"My kite is gonna sail the highest and longest at the kite festival next week," said Addy, beaming.

"I'm sure it'll do fine," said Poppa. "But it ain't going nowhere without a frame. You ready for the wood now?"

"I'm ready," said Addy.

"I'm ready," Esther repeated, climbing over Sam and plopping down next to Addy.

"No, you can't help me, Esther," insisted Addy. She tried to pick Esther up and move her away.

"No!" screamed Esther. "I want to help."

"Now, you be nice to your sister, Addy," Momma said.

Addy let go. "I'm being nice to her," Addy said. "But she already knotted up some of my string and glued her fingers together."

"Addy, give me a piece of paper. I'll draw with her," Sam said. "Come here," he said, coaxing Esther back to him.

Poppa handed Addy the wood. She had to slide her paper under the table to make room.

"I can't wait until we move into our new place at the end of the month," Momma said. "We gonna have much more space."

Earlier in the week, the family had looked at the new apartment. Addy could hardly believe it. Two whole rooms! The apartment had a stove, so Momma could make their meals. There were four long windows that let in plenty of sunlight. The rent would cost an extra three dollars a month. With Poppa, Momma, and Sam working, they could afford it, but there wouldn't be any extra money. Addy loved the new apartment, but worried about leaving her boarding house friends.

"I'm gonna miss M'dear and the Goldens," Addy said now.

"We only moving a few blocks away," said Momma. "You can come back and visit whenever you want."

"It won't be the same," sighed Addy. She made a cross of the two pieces of

wood and began binding them together
with string.

"Wait," Poppa said. "Your frame ain't
square." He got down on the floor next to
Addy. "It's a little crooked." Poppa shifted
the wood and held it while Addy tied the
frame together.

Addy pulled the paper out and

began gluing it to the frame. She was almost done when Esther got up and tripped over the frame, bending it and tearing the paper.

"Look what you done!" Addy yelled. "You ruined it!"

"Sorry, Addy," said Esther, backing away. "It broke."

"And you broke it! You mess up everything!" cried Addy.

"Addy, that's enough," Momma scolded. "Put that kite up and come here to me."

Addy placed her bent kite on her bed and sank into a chair next to Momma.

"I don't like you talking to your

sister like that. She didn't mean to step on your kite," Momma said. She was holding Esther on her lap.

"Momma, she don't never mean to do stuff, but she do it," Addy complained. "She go through my school sack, break my slate pencils. Last week she tore a page out my speller."

"Oh, Addy, your sister love you, and she touch your things because she want to be *like* you," explained Momma. "She want to be a big girl and go to school like you do."

"I'm a big girl," said Esther.

"You ain't. You a baby," said Addy.

"She *is* a baby, so you got to be

patient with her," said Momma. "She don't know better. You got to put your school sack away where she can't get it."

"Well, maybe that'll be something good about us moving," said Addy. "I'll have more room to keep my things from Esther."

"You gonna have a room to go in and do your school lessons, too," Momma said.

"That's right," Sam said. "You keep up with them high marks you getting, and you gonna end up a teacher like you want."

Addy smiled. "I hope so," she said. She gave Esther a hug. "The kite festival ain't until Wednesday. I can get the kite done before then, if Esther leave it alone."

✸

At the end of the school day on Monday, Addy and the other children were packing up their sacks when Miss Dunn asked for their attention.

"I know you boys and girls are excited about the kite festival on Wednesday," Miss Dunn said. "Let's hope for a windy day."

Harriet, Addy's desk partner, whispered to Addy, "My kite is going to be the best. My father had it made for me out of expensive white paper. It's going to float above everybody else's like a butterfly." Harriet fluttered her fingers.

"It ain't gonna be the best because it cost the most," Addy whispered back. "My poppa ain't have somebody make my kite. He helped me."

Addy was startled when Miss Dunn clapped her hands together sharply.

"Addy," Miss Dunn said. "I need to see you after school."

Addy slid down in her seat. It wasn't fair! Harriet had started it, and now Addy was the one being kept after school. Glancing at Harriet, Addy saw a crooked smirk on her face.

"You, too, Harriet," Miss Dunn said. "I need to see you after school as well."

"But, Miss Dunn, I didn't do anything," Harriet protested.

11

"That's enough, Harriet," Miss Dunn said. "The rest of you are dismissed."

It was Addy who smirked this time. At least Harriet had gotten caught, too.

After all the other students were gone, Miss Dunn called Harriet and Addy up to her desk. She had a stern look on her face.

"I want you girls to know, I didn't keep you after school for talking, though I could have," Miss Dunn said. Then she smiled. "You girls have had a wonderful year of studies. That's why I've recommended you both for the Institute for Colored Youth for the fall!"

Addy and Harriet squealed in delight.

"I've recommended you both for the Institute for
Colored Youth for the fall!"

"Miss Dunn, you serious?" asked
Addy.

"I most certainly am," replied Miss
Dunn. She handed each girl a letter.
"I want each of you to take this home,"
Miss Dunn said. "Give it to your parents.
It explains more about the school.
Congratulations."

Addy walked away from Miss Dunn's
desk shaky with excitement. Ever since
she had heard about the Institute for
Colored Youth, the I.C.Y., she'd dreamt

 of going there. The I.C.Y trained
black students to be teachers.
She would be a *teacher,* just
like Miss Dunn!

With the letter grasped tightly in her

hand, Addy grabbed her school sack. She couldn't wait to tell everybody the good news. She raced down the school steps, leaping off the third step from the bottom and flying into the air. Then she took off running down the street.

"Wait for me!" Harriet called.

Addy had not even seen her. She stopped and carefully placed the letter inside one of her books while she waited for Harriet.

"Isn't it great that we'll be going to the I.C.Y.?" Harriet exclaimed.

"It seem like a dream," Addy said.

"I always knew I would get in," said Harriet. "I am the smartest student in the class."

"One of the smartest," Addy said.

"Well, the truth is," said Harriet, "I'm glad you're going, too. I'll have to work my hardest to stay ahead of you."

Addy smiled. Coming from Harriet, that was a compliment. As the girls approached a corner, Harriet said, "Let's walk by the I.C.Y.! It's only a few blocks from here."

When they came to the small brick building that was the I.C.Y., Harriet said, "My family knows Mr. Bassett, the principal. He was at our house for dinner last week, and he said education is the only way colored people will get ahead. My parents told him the cost of attending the I.C.Y. is well worth it."

"What cost?" asked Addy. "Miss Dunn didn't say nothing about any cost."

"Oh, it does. Ten dollars a year," Harriet said confidently. "Mr. Bassett said the Quakers used to fund the school, but now colored people are paying for it. Well, I've got to get on home. You want to walk with me?" asked Harriet.

Addy shook her head and mumbled, "I'm going the other way." She waited while Harriet skipped off down the block. With a trembling hand, she pulled out the letter and slowly lifted the wax seal. Her heart racing, she read the letter quickly. She came to a dead stop right in the middle. "The cost of ten dollars a year can be met . . ."

Ten dollars! Addy thought. *There ain't no way Momma and Poppa can afford that, not with us moving to a new apartment. Why did Harriet have to be right?*

Addy crumpled up the letter and stuffed it in her sack. There was no point in rushing to tell anyone the news. She would give the letter to Momma and Poppa maybe after they moved. With her head down, Addy set off for home.

☀

On Wednesday, Addy sat at her desk, gazing out the window. It was windy, and the trees, with their bright new leaves of green, swayed before the window. It would have been a great day to fly a kite, but it was raining and showed no signs of letting up. Every now and then there was a grumble of thunder, and a flash of light brightened the sky.

A boy raised his hand. "Miss Dunn, can we fly our kites anyway? We can do like Benjamin Franklin did when he discovered electricity," he said.

"No," Miss Dunn said. "We won't be tying keys to our kite strings and going out in the rain. It's too dangerous. The kite festival must be postponed until tomorrow."

Addy looked at the kites lined up in front of the room. Harriet's stood out from the rest. It was all white with a long white tail. It looked perfect, like it could sail all the way to the moon. Addy's kite was next to Harriet's. The frame was a bit lopsided, not quite square, Poppa would say. It had a tail of many colors. There was a piece of brown cloth from one of Sam's old shirts, scraps of red left over from dresses Momma made for Addy and Esther, and black strips from when Momma had hemmed a pair of Poppa's pants. Addy sighed and rested her face in her hands. *Harriet was right*, Addy thought. *Her kite is the best. Mine won't stand a chance against hers.*

At recess later that morning, Harriet caught her by the arm.

"My parents have an appointment for us to tour the I.C.Y.," said Harriet.

Addy sighed and rested her face in her hands.

"When are you and your parents going?"

Addy paused before she answered. She remembered reading something in the letter about a visit for parents.

"Oh, we going on Saturday when they get off work," Addy said. She couldn't look at Harriet. She felt bad about lying.

"That's great," Harriet said. "That's when we're going. I told Miss Dunn this morning, and she'll be there, too. She can introduce us to all the teachers, even though I don't really need to be introduced because I'm sure Mr. Bassett has told them all about me."

Addy went to the back of the room where Miss Dunn kept a crock of cool water and took a long drink. She watched as Harriet joined a group of her friends. Harriet did work hard, but things also came easily to her, good things. She was smart, and had so many friends. Her family had money. Even though Harriet liked to brag, she wasn't a bad person. She would make a good teacher.

But for Addy the dream was over. She knew she must destroy the letter she had crumpled up. It would only make her parents feel bad because they couldn't afford to send her. She would make up an excuse on Monday to tell Harriet and Miss Dunn about why she hadn't come to the I.C.Y. on Saturday. Addy would be ashamed if everyone at

school knew her family was too poor
to pay the money, not when ten dollars
didn't seem to be anything to Harriet's
family. Back at her seat, Addy looked
through her school sack for the letter,
but it was gone.

☀

At dinner that night, Addy sat next
to Sam, pushing chicken and dumplings
around her plate. For dessert, Mrs.
Golden had made a huge blackberry
cobbler, but Addy only poked at its
shiny top crusted with sugar, and was
surprised when Poppa stood up and
tapped his glass with a fork to get the
attention of the Goldens, M'dear, and

the other boarders.

"I got a announcement to make," Poppa said. "As most of you know, me and my family had planned on moving out at the end of the month, but there's been a change of plans. We gonna be staying on here for at least another year."

Addy looked at Poppa. This was news to her.

"Our Addy is going to the I.C.Y. in the fall. She gonna be a teacher!" Poppa said in a booming voice.

Everyone clapped, and Addy looked over at Momma, who was smiling and crying all at the same time. Addy was stunned. Before she knew what was happening, she was being hugged by

everybody, kissed by everybody. All the
while she was wondering how Poppa
had found out.

When the family went upstairs after
dinner, Momma pulled out the crumpled
 letter from Miss Dunn.

"Where did you get it?"
asked Addy.

"Esther. She gave it to me this morning after you left for school," Momma said. "Honey, why did you try to hide it from us?"

Addy explained, "I ain't think we could afford it. Momma, ten dollars is more than you make in two months. I was shamed to tell Harriet and Miss Dunn that we poor."

"We *is* poor," Sam said. "There ain't no shame in that. We work hard for our money, like you work hard at your lessons. You should have told us about the school."

Poppa kneeled down next to Addy. "We all proud of you, and whatever it take for you to go to the I.C.Y., we gonna do it."

"We'll be all right in the boarding house. We together here, a family. That's what matter," Momma said.

"Come here," Addy called to her sister, who was down on the floor writing on Addy's slate.

Esther sprang up. "See, I write like you, Addy," she said.

"I see," Addy said, looking at the scribbles Esther had made. She gave Esther a hug. "Thanks for wanting to be like me."

❋

The next day at school, the weather was perfect for the kite festival. A strong wind blew steadily. Sailing in a patch of clear blue sky, one kite flew high above all the others. It was a little lopsided and had a tail of many colors. Addy stood far, far below it, letting out more and more string from the spool. She smiled proudly and glanced over to where Harriet was trying to sail her kite. All day, it had never gotten more than a few feet off the ground before it crashed.

"I can help you," Addy called to Harriet.

"I don't need any help," Harriet said. Then she sighed loudly. "Yes, I do."

Addy handed Harriet her spool, so she could see what was wrong with Harriet's kite.

"I think the tail too long. It's heavy," Addy said. "If it's trimmed, I think it'll fly good."

"I believe you," Harriet said. "You must know something about kites."

Addy smiled, and snapped off half of Harriet's kite tail. Then she took off running, faster and faster as the kite lifted up, dipped slightly, and then began sailing upward. It pulled and tugged at the string as it rose higher. Rushing back to Harriet, Addy handed Harriet her kite and took her own back.

Harriet said, "You have the best kite here. How did you get yours to fly so high?"

"My family," Addy said. "Together we sail."

"What does that mean?" asked Harriet.

"Everything," Addy said, taking off to race in the wind with her kite. "I'll see you on Saturday at the I.C.Y."

CONNIE PORTER

At 9   Now

When I was growing up, my family did not have much money. Yet I don't remember feeling ashamed the way Addy did at first. My parents always taught me that who you are is more important than what you have. Today, I often tell children the same thing.

Connie Porter is the author of the Addy books in The American Girls Collection.

LOOKING BACK 1864

A PEEK INTO
THE PAST

**TEACHING
IN
1864**

The Institute for Colored Youth,
known as the I.C.Y., was the first high
school for African Americans.

It was founded in 1837
by the Society of Friends.
The Society of Friends,
also known as the Quakers,
is a religious group that
works for peace. It was
among the first to organize
abolition societies, or groups
against slavery. The I.C.Y.'s mission was
to train African American teachers
through other African American teachers.

*The I.C.Y. in
Philadelphia*

A classroom in 1910

The I.C.Y. was also important to the Philadelphia community. The large library loaned books to students and the general public. The school sponsored speakers like Frederick Douglass. He was a former slave who devoted his life to the

Frederick Douglass

abolition of slavery and the fight for black rights.

To be admitted to the I.C.Y., children had to be at least 11 years old and take an exam for reading, writing, and math. Once they were accepted, they took classes in history, geography, grammar, Latin, algebra, philosophy, and chemistry.

Being accepted into the I.C.Y. was an exciting opportunity for African American girls and boys in Addy's time. It was one of the few schools in America where black students could get an excellent education—thanks in part to one of its teachers, Fanny Jackson Coppin.

Schoolbooks from the 1860s

Fanny was a remarkable woman and teacher. In 1869 she was named principal of the I.C.Y.—the first African American school principal ever. But this achievement was only a small part of what made her so special.

Fanny Jackson Coppin

Like Addy, Fanny was raised in slavery. Her aunt Sarah, who earned only six dollars a month, saved $125 to buy Fanny's freedom. As a girl, Fanny worked hard to educate herself. By the time she was a teenager, she had one dream: "To get an education and teach my people."

In 1860, Fanny enrolled in Oberlin College, in Ohio, where she was a top student. While she was going to school, she organized classes for newly freed slaves, gave private music lessons, and became the college's first black student teacher. After graduation, she went to the I.C.Y. to teach—and soon became one of its most popular teachers.

By the end of Fanny's first year at the I.C.Y., the number of girls who attended the high school nearly doubled—from 42 students to 80 students. Fanny was a popular teacher because she made learning easy and enjoyable.

Fanny's students loved the stories and poems she made up to teach every-

A school for newly freed people

thing from the Ten Commandments to
the parts of speech. One of Fanny's
favorite teaching poems began:

> A noun is the name of anything,
> As school, or garden, hoop, or swing.
> Adjectives tell the kind of noun,
> As great, small, pretty, white, or
> brown.

Fanny encouraged her students to help one another. She urged I.C.Y. graduates to teach, especially in the South, where it had been against the law for black people to go to school.

While Fanny was principal, she thought that the I.C.Y. should teach students trades, too. In Philadelphia in the 1880s, more jobs were becoming available for carpenters, bricklayers, shoe-makers, printers, dressmakers, and cooks. African Americans were not able to get these jobs because they did not have the training.

Carpentry students learning how to construct a staircase

Fanny and the school raised $40,000, and in 1889 the Industrial Department opened at the I.C.Y. The classes were flooded with more applicants than they had room for! There were over 400 applicants for the program.

Fanny retired from the I.C.Y. in 1902. Throughout her 37 years there, Fanny lived by her motto: "If one wants to learn a thing, teach it to another."

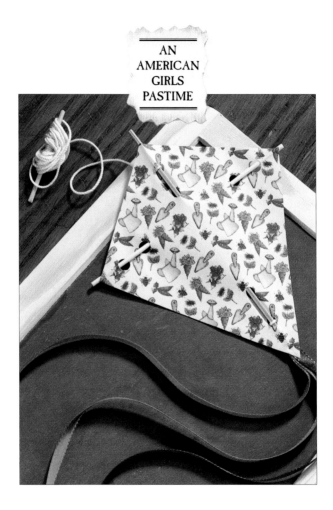

AN
AMERICAN
GIRLS
PASTIME

MAKE A MINI KITE

Fly a kite and let your dreams soar!

Addy discovered that it takes many things to build a kite that can fly. None of the things can fly by themselves, but together they make something that can. Addy realized this was true about her dreams, too. Without her family's help, she wouldn't have been able to go to the I.C.Y. and fulfill her dream of becoming a teacher. Let your own dreams soar with a mini kite.

You Will Need:

Brown or patterned wrapping
paper, 5 by 6 inches

Pencil

Scissors

Hole punch

Bamboo skewer, 6 inches long

Bamboo skewer, 5 inches long

Ruler, 6 inches long

Thin string

Bamboo skewer, 2 inches long

Glue

Thin ribbon, 12 inches long

1. Fold your paper in half lengthwise.
   Draw half of the kite shape as shown.
   Cut out the shape, and open it up.

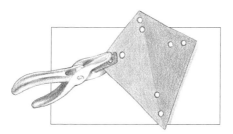

2. Use the hole punch to punch 8
   holes in the kite shape as shown.

3. Carefully weave the bamboo skewers in and out of the holes as shown below. The 6-inch skewer should be the vertical spine, and the 5-inch skewer should be the horizontal spine.

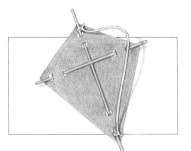

4. Cut a 10-inch piece of string. Tie it to the vertical spine as shown. This string is called the bridle.

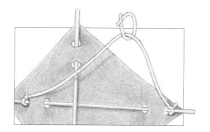

5. Tie a small loop of string to the bridle.

6. Cut a 6-foot piece of string. Wind the string around the 2-inch skewer until there are 6 inches left. This string is the flying line.

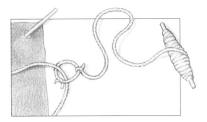

7. Tie the end of the flying line to the loop on the bridle.

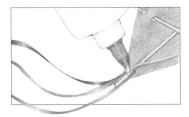

8. Glue the ribbon to the bottom of the kite for a tail, and your kite is ready to fly!

THE AMERICAN GIRLS COLLECTION®

To learn more about The American Girls Collection, fill out the postcard below and mail it to American Girl, or call **1-800-845-0005**. We'll send you a free catalogue full of books, dolls, dresses, and other delights for girls.

I'm an American girl who loves to get mail. Please send me a catalogue of The American Girls Collection:

My name is _____

My address is _____

City _____ State _____ Zip _____

My birth date is ____/____/____
             Month Day Year

And send a catalogue to my friend:

My friend's name is _____

Address _____

City _____ State _____ Zip _____
      1961

      1225